**The Urbana Free Library**

To renew: call **217-367-4057**
or go to **urbanafreelibrary.org**
and select **My Account**

# DEAR MOON

Stephen
Wunderli

Illustrator
Maria Luisa
Di Gravio

Published by Familius LLC, www.familius.com
1254 Commerce Way, Sanger, CA 93657

Familius books are available at special discounts for bulk purchases, whether for sales promotions or for family or corporate use. For more information, contact Familius Sales at 559-876-2170 or email orders@familius.com.

Library of Congress Control Number: 2020939033

Print ISBN: 9781641702690
Ebook ISBN: 9781641703710
KF: 9781641703956
FE: 9781641704199

Printed in China

Edited by Michele Robbins and Brooke Jorden

Cover design by Maria Luisa Di Gravio
Book design by Carlos Guerrero

10 9 8 7 6 5 4 3 2 1

First Edition

"It just keeps moving," Max says.
"And then another day comes."

"We could try and stop it," Ely suggests.
"Then I won't have to leave so soon."

"We want to have a word with you!"
Max shouts at the moon. "Face-to-face,
man-to-Man in the Moon. We need you to stay
where you are!"

"You think we can make him stay put?" Ely asks.

Max glares at the moon. "I have a plan."

"This is going to work!" Max shouts.

Max and Ely launch into the night
beyond the trees and the stars
to lasso the moon.

Almost.

BLASTOFF!

"We tried," Ely says. "Thanks anyway. I guess there's no stopping the moon or the next day from coming or me going to the hospital . . ."

"We're not giving up," Max says. "I have another plan. These bicycle tubes should do the trick."

"Got you now!" Ely yells. "Nobody messes with my best friend, Max!"

Oh no.

"NOW YOU'VE DONE IT, MOON! STOP!" shouts Max.

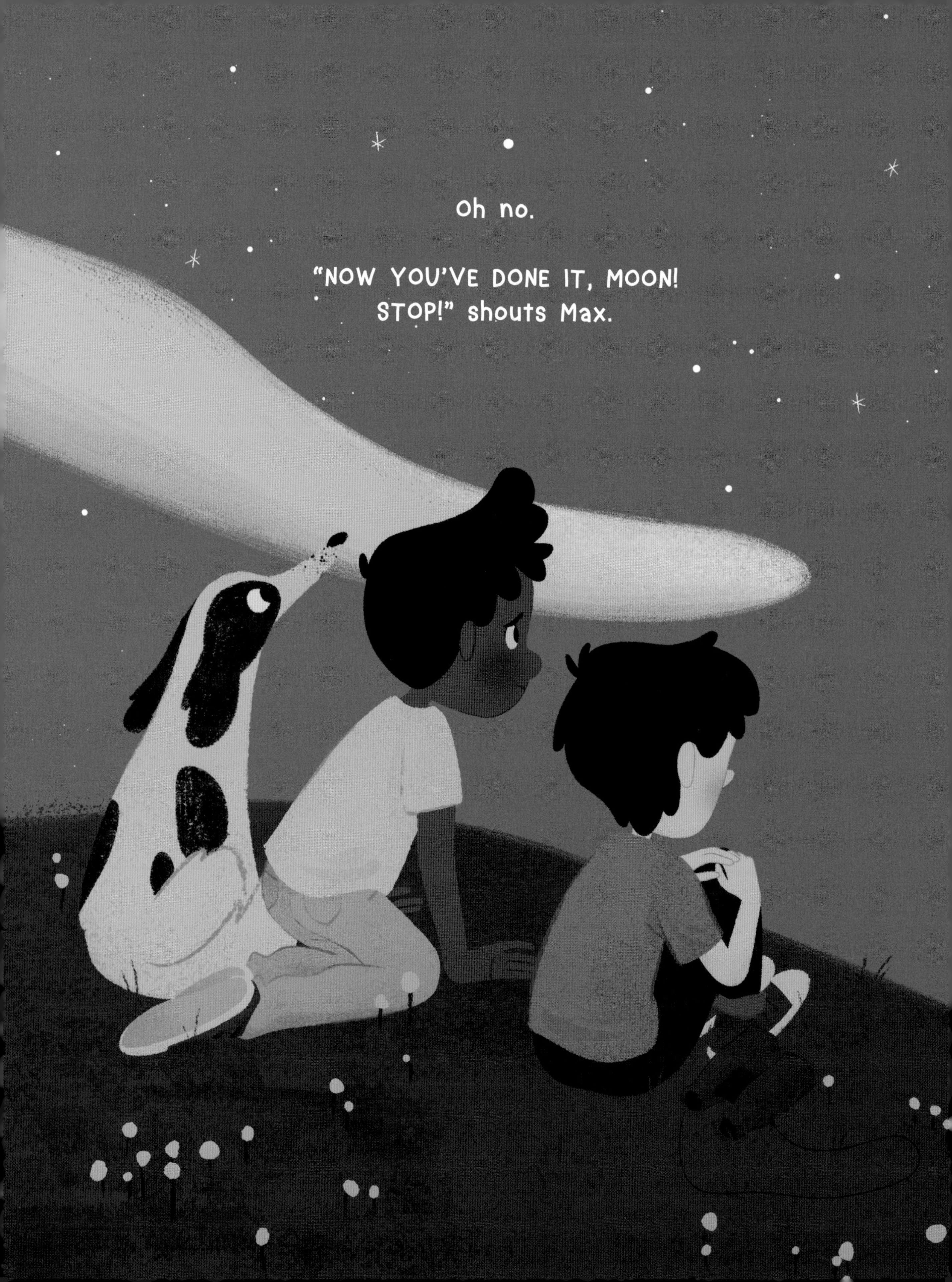

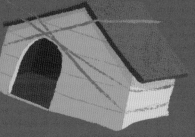

"Thanks for trying," Ely says.
"But I don't think the moon ever stops."

"I won't give up," Max says.
"Not even 'til the end of the end of the very end of the world."

"I wish you could go with me to the hospital,"
whispers Ely.

"Me too," Max says. "Are you afraid?"

"A little," says Ely.

"You want me to be afraid for you
so you don't have to?" asks Max.

"Okay," says Ely. "Thanks."

The early morning moon is watching.
Somehow it seems closer to Max
and Ely than the hospital.

Ely looks at it one last time.
"See you soon, Moon."

Max marches home.
He has a new plan.

If the moon won't stop, maybe I can make it
move faster! thinks Max.

"Better run, Moon. I will scare you!
Go, Moon, go! And don't come back without Ely!"

It's no use. The moon moves along same as always.
Same. Same. Same.

One night, the moon is so close Max
can almost touch it.

"Okay," says Max.
"No more scaring. Let's be friends.
Can you see Ely from up there?
I know you can. Is he OK?
Does he hurt? Does he miss me?
Will you make sure he comes home?"

The moon glows a little more.

Sometimes it's hard to understand the moon.

# WELCOME BACK EL Y

The nights go by. The day arrives.
Ely rolls out with a new haircut.

"Cool," says Max. "Your head looks like the moon."

"My eyebrows are gone, too,
and my new wheelchair has a motor.
RRRRRRRZZZZZZZZ," sputters Ely as he spins in circles.

"I had a word with the moon," says Max.
"I told him to make sure you are okay."

Ely smiles. "I think I'll be seeing him in person soon."

"I'm going with you," Max says.
"We'll build a new rocket with super blasters."

Max and Ely make the
best rocket ever.

It takes a long time.

BUMP!
The rocket nudges the sleepy moon.

Ely walks onto the moon and waves goodbye.
The moon glows brighter.

The rocket floats back down to earth,
landing safely with Max on board.

Max puts on his favorite mask and cries
the sadness out. It takes some time.
Then he shoots a note to the moon.